CHARLOTTE
AND QUIET PLACE
THE

CHARLOTTE
AND THE QUIET PLACE
THE

DEBORAH SOSIN

ILLUSTRATED BY SARA WOOLLEY

Plum
Blossom
Books

Charlotte's house is noisy.

In the hallway,
the floorboards groan.

In the living room,
the TV bellows and blares.

In the kitchen, her dog, Otto, yips, yaps, and yowls.

Even in her bedroom, which is
supposed to be a quiet place,
the old steam radiator
hisses, whistles, and whines.

Where can Charlotte
find a quiet place?

Charlotte's school is noisy.

In the classroom, the bell clangs.

In the lunchroom,
the trays clatter and crash.

On the playground,
the swings creak, squeak,
and rattle.

Even in the library, which is supposed to be a quiet place, the children giggle, yammer, and yell.

Where can Charlotte find a quiet place?

Charlotte's neighborhood is very, very noisy.

On the sidewalk, the jackhammers blast.

On the street, the sirens warble and wail.

Underground, the subway
screeches, rumbles, and roars.

Even in the park, which is
supposed to be a quiet place, the
leaf blower buzzes, blusters, and hums.

"Nooo!"

cries Charlotte.

"I have to find a quiet place!"

One Saturday morning,
Charlotte takes Otto for a walk.

In the park, Otto spots a squirrel and he lurches free.

Charlotte chases Otto, charging,
charging down the hill,
over the bridge, and

into a grove, where
Otto skids to a stop.

Charlotte and Otto are out of breath.

hoo ahh
hoo ahh *hoo ahh*
hoo ahh

Together, they sit down to rest.

They close their eyes.

Charlotte's belly rises up and down,

up and down.

hooo ahhh hooo ahhh hooo ahhh

Her breath goes in and out, in and out.

hoooo ahhh hoooo ahhhh

Her mind slows down.

hoooo ahhhh

It is quiet, at last.

It is so, so quiet, Charlotte notices
an even quieter place,

a place deep in her belly, where her
breath is soft and even,

a place deep in her mind, where her
thoughts are hushed and low,

a place as quiet as the small silence on the
very last page of her favorite book,

the silence right after "The End."

When Charlotte is ready, she and Otto
hike slowly away from the grove,

back over the bridge, and
up the hill toward home.

Nowadays, Charlotte's house is still noisy,

her school is still noisy,

and her neighborhood is still very, very noisy.

But Charlotte remembers that day in the park.
So wherever she is,
whenever she wants,
when her world is too noisy,
Charlotte simply closes her eyes and travels
back to that peaceful place—

the place deep in her belly, where her
breath is soft and even,

hoooooooo ahhhhhh

the place deep in her mind, where her
thoughts are hushed and low,

hoooooooo ahhhhhh

the quiet place inside.

For Nicholas and Mollie, my nephew and niece. May you always find a quiet place inside. —D.S.

For my students past, present, and future. Thank you for the wealth of creativity and inspiration. —S.W.

Plum Blossom Books, the children's imprint of Parallax Press, publishes books on mindfulness for young people and the grown-ups in their lives.

Parallax Press
P.O. Box 7355
Berkeley, California 94707
parallax.org

Cover and interior design by Debbie Berne

Library of Congress Cataloging-in-Publication Data is available upon request.

FSC® MIX Paper from responsible sources FSC® C111080 www.fsc.org

1 2 3 4 5 / 19 18 17 16 15

"What better way to prepare children for our busy world? Adults and children will want to read it together again and again, and breathe."
—CHRISTOPHER GERMER, PhD, *The Mindful Path to Self-Compassion*

"Thank you, Charlotte, for helping children and adults discover the stillness and quiet that is always alive inside each one of us. Hoooo ahhhh!"
—AMY SALTZMAN, MD, *A Still Quiet Place*